Hello, Family Members,

Learning to read is one of the most important accomplishments of early childhood. **Hello Reader!** books are designed to help children become skilled readers who like to read. Beginning readers learn to read by remembering frequently used words like "the," "is," and "and"; by using phonics skills to decode new words; and by interpreting picture and text clues. These books provide both the stories children enjoy and the structure they need to read fluently and independently. Here are suggestions for helping your child.

- Have your child think about a word he or she does not recognize right away. Provide hints such as "Let's see if we know the sounds" and "Have we read other words like this one?"
- Encourage your child to use phonics skills to sound out new words.
- Provide the word for your child when more assistance is needed so that he or she does not struggle and the experience of reading with you is a positive one.
- Encourage your child to have fun by reading with a lot of expression...like an actor!

I do hope that you and your child enjoy this book.

—Francie Alexander
Chief Education Officer,
Scholastic's Learning Ventures

Activity Pages

In the back of the book are skill-building activities. These are designed to give children further reading and comprehension practice and to provide added enjoyment. Offer help with directions as needed and encourage your child to have FUN with each activity.

Game Cards

In the middle of the book are eight pairs of game cards. These are designed to help your child become more familiar with words in the book and to play fun games.

• Have your child use the word cards to find matching words in the story. Then have him or her use the picture cards to find matching words in the story.

• Play a matching game. Here's how: Place the cards face up. Have your child match words to pictures. Once the child feels confident matching words to pictures, put cards face down. Have the child lift one card, then lift a second card to see if both match. If the cards match, the child can keep them. If not, place the cards face down once again. Keep going until he or she finds all matches.

ISBN: 0-439-17934-3

Library of Congress Cataloging-in-Publication Data available

10   9   8   7   6   5   4   3   04   05

Printed in the U.S.A. 23
First printing, March 2002

Wiggly Worm

by Wendy Cheyette Lewison
Illustrated by Judith Moffatt

My First Hello Reader!
With Game Cards

SCHOLASTIC INC. Cartwheel ·B·O·O·K·S·®

New York Toronto London Auckland Sydney
Mexico City New Delhi Hong Kong Buenos Aires

How does a worm walk? Do you know? How does it get where it wants to go?

Does it walk with a hop
like a kangaroo?

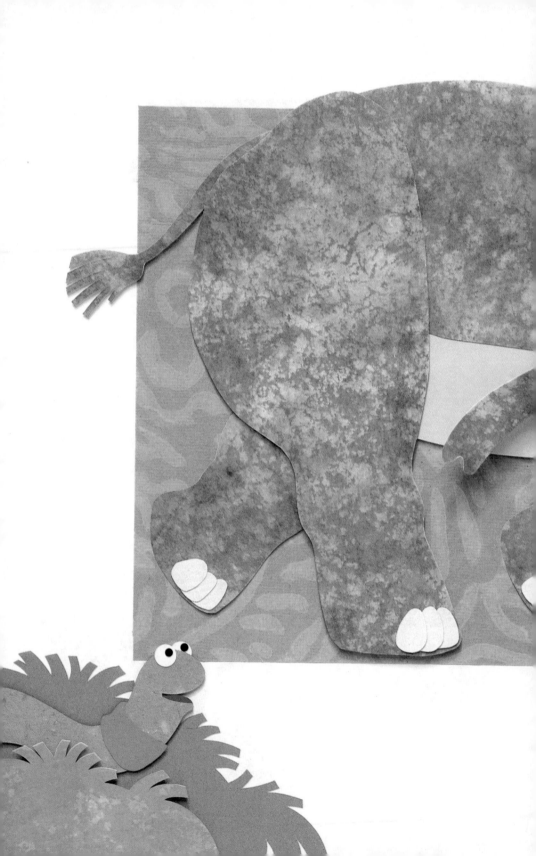

Does it walk like an elephant
at the zoo?

Or do worms walk
like doggies do?

How does a worm walk?
Can you say?

How does it go
its wormy way?

Does it walk with a waddle
like a downy duck?

Does it walk
like a chicken

with a cluck, cluck, cluck?

Does a worm walk fast—
or very slow?

Let's find a worm,
and then we'll know.

Hold out your hands.

Put the worm on.

THAT's how a worm walks!

Wiggle, wiggle . . .

. . . GONE!

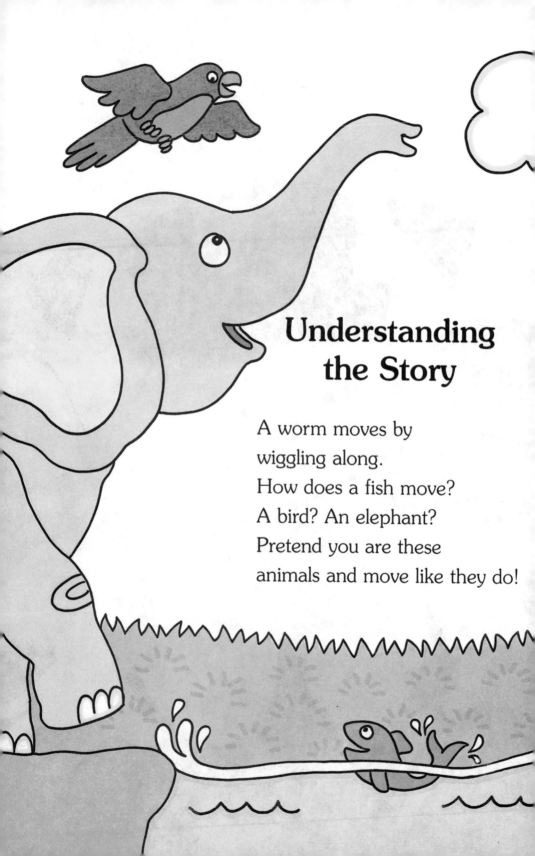

Understanding the Story

A worm moves by
wiggling along.
How does a fish move?
A bird? An elephant?
Pretend you are these
animals and move like they do!

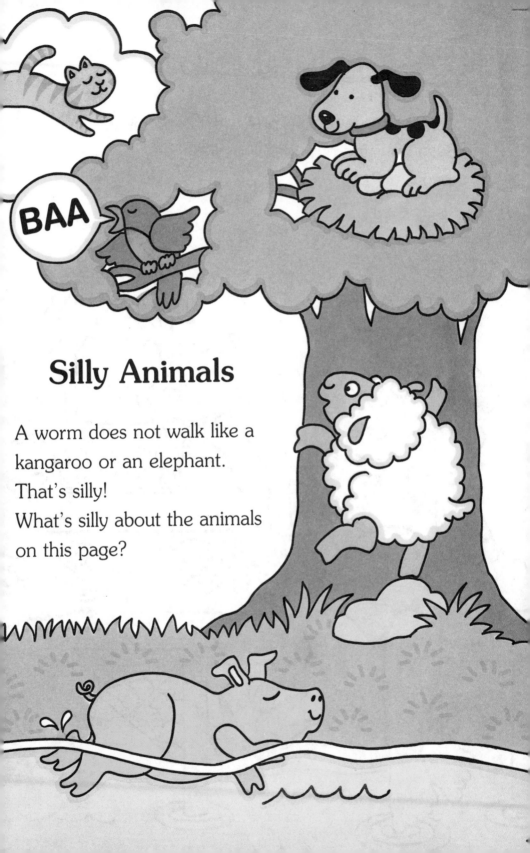

Silly Animals

A worm does not walk like a
kangaroo or an elephant.
That's silly!
What's silly about the animals
on this page?

W Is for "Worm"

The word "worm" starts with the letter W.
Can you find nine other pictures whose names
begin with W?

Rhyme Time

This story has many words that rhyme.

Draw a line to match the words that rhyme.

slow	say
zoo	cluck
way	know
duck	you

Wiggly Worms

Worms wiggle into all kinds of shapes!
Can you find the two worms that are exactly
alike in each row?

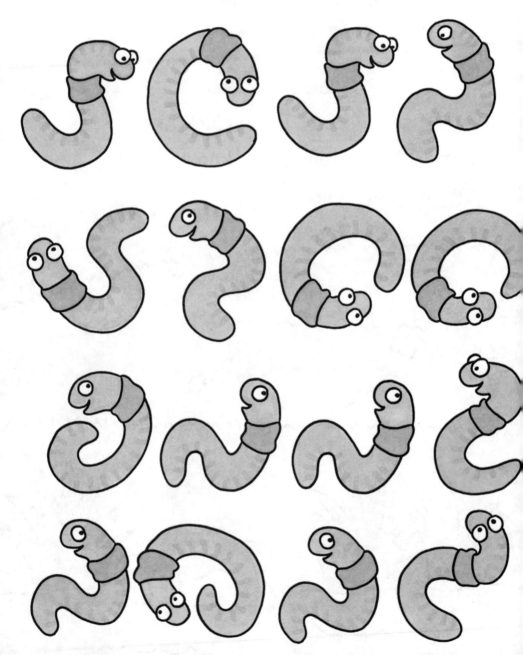

A Can of Worms

How many wiggly worms are in the can?
Can you count them?

Understanding the Story

A fish swishes its fins.

A bird flies by flapping its wings.

An elephant walks on four legs.

Silly Animals

Cats don't fly.

Sheep can't climb trees.

Birds don't say, "*BAA.*"

Dogs don't hatch eggs.

Pigs can't swim like fish.

Rhyme Time

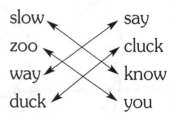

slow — say
zoo — cluck
way — know
duck — you

W Is for "Worm"

These words begin with W: witch, wand, wagon, wheels, web, water, watermelon, well, watch

Wiggly Worms

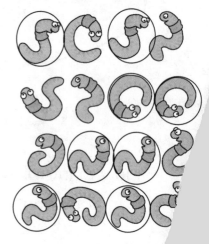

A Can of Worms

There are ten worms in the can.